THE NUTCRACKER

A DK PUBLISHING BOOK
www.dk.com

To Gabriel
J. M.

To Sita
D. C-D.

A RETELLING FOR YOUNG READERS

Produced by Leapfrog Press Ltd

Project Editor Lizzy Bacon
Art Editor Penny Lamprell

For DK Publishing
Senior Editor Alastair Dougall
Managing Art Editor Jacquie Gulliver
Picture Research Liz Moore
Production Steve Lang

First American Edition, 1999

2 4 6 8 10 9 7 5 3
Published in the United States by
DK Publishing, Inc., 95 Madison Avenue
New York, New York 10016

Text and compilation copyright © 1999 Dorling Kindersley Limited
Illustrations copyright © 1999 James Mayhew

Library of Congress Cataloging-in-Publication Data
Clement-Davies, David, 1961–
    The nutcracker / by Ernst Hoffmann : adapted by David Clement
-Davies. --1st American ed.
      p.   cm. -- (Eyewitness classics)
    Summary: After hearing how the toy nutcracker that she and her
brother received for Christmas got his ugly face, Marie helps break
the spell he is under and watches him change into a handsome prince.
Illustrated notes throughout the text explain the historical
background of the story.
  ISBN 0-7894-4766-5
   [1. Fairy tales.]   I. Hoffmann. E. T. A. (Ernst Theodor Amadeus).
1776–1822. Nussknacker und Mausekönig. II. Title. III. Series.
PZ8.C5578Nu 1999
[Fic]--dc21   99–34274
                                              CIP

Color reproduction by Bright Arts in Hong Kong

Printed by Graphicom in Italy

THE NUTCRACKER

ERNST HOFFMANN

Adapted by
DAVID
CLEMENT-DAVIES

Illustrated by
JAMES
MAYHEW

DK Publishing, Inc.

Marie

Fritz

Nutcracker

Drosselmeier

Mama

Papa

CONTENTS

INTRODUCTION 6

A MERRY CHRISTMAS 8

GERMAN TOYS 10

Chapter one
CHRISTMAS EVE 12

Chapter two
THE PRESENTS 14

Chapter three
MARIE'S PET 16

Chapter four
WONDERFUL EVENTS 18

Chapter five
THE BATTLE 22

Chapter six
THE INVALID 26

Chapter seven
THE STORY OF PIRLIPAT 28

Chapter eight
DROSSELMEIER CONTINUES 34

Chapter nine
CRACKATOOK 38

Chapter ten
UNCLE AND NEPHEW 42

Chapter eleven
VICTORY 46

Chapter twelve
LAND OF SWEETS 50

Chapter thirteen
THE METROPOLIS 54

Chapter fourteen
CONCLUSION 58

FROM BOOK TO BALLET 60

HOFFMANN AND HIS TIMES 62

The astrologer

The clockmaker

Drosselmeier's nephew

The king

The queen

Dame Mouserink

INTRODUCTION

The Nutcracker brings to mind dancing soldiers and sugarplum fairies. Tchaikovsky's enchanting ballet was based on *The Nutcracker and the Mouse King*, written in 1816 by the German Romantic Ernst Hoffmann, composer, writer, and author. Retold in this beautifully illustrated edition, *The Nutcracker* is an extraordinary modern fairy-tale.

The events of Christmas Eve in the Stahlbaum household turn into a wonderful adventure for a little girl. Fantasy becomes an alternative reality as the reader accompanies Marie on a journey initiated by love and admiration. Hoffmann's memorable creation, the disturbing but humorous Godpapa Drosselmeier, is there to guide her.

Hoffmann lived in the powerful German state of Prussia during the Napoleonic Wars (1799-1815). The historical and cultural context of the story is explored in margin notes and information pages. The reader can revel in a German Christmas, delight in the ingenuity of German toys, and learn of the wartorn yet culturally flourishing times in which the author lived.

Hoffmann's main theme is the search for the beauty of truth in a world where the ugliness of evil challenges the child at every turn. This Eyewitness Classic captures the magical poetry of a story which inspired Tchaikovsky's universally loved ballet.

A scene from The English National Ballet's 1998 production of *The Nutcracker*.

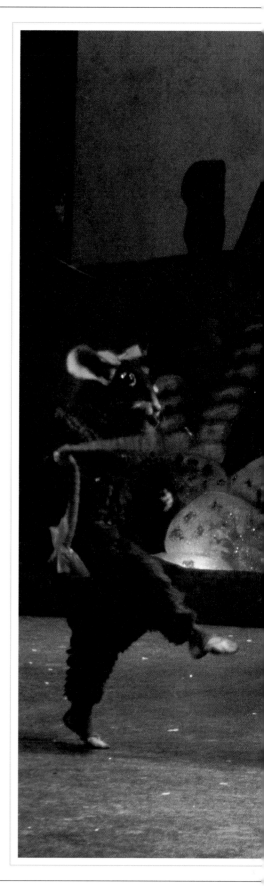

A MERRY CHRISTMAS

Christmas in Germany in the early 19th century was a special time. Children like Marie and Fritz in the story celebrated "Martinmas" in November to welcome in the festive season. In December, families went to Christmas fairs to buy Christmas trees and food. They noticed mysterious things happening from St. Nicholas's Day, December 6th. Adults whispered together, rooms in the house were locked. Then, on Christmas Eve, the children saw the Christmas tree, beautifully decorated. They knew that the Christ child or Santa Claus had brought them the gifts that lay under the tree.

People dressed up as St. Nicholas to give children presents on St. Nicholas's Eve, December 5th.

St. Nicholas
St. Nicholas was the patron saint of children. Some children received gifts on his feast day, as well as Christmas.

The Christ child
Just like Marie and Fritz, children discovered that the Christ child brought them presents if they were good. They left wishlists for Him on the windowsill.

Santa Claus decorations were becoming popular.

Santa Claus
In Hoffmann's time, children in northern Germany believed that Santa Claus, not the Christ child, brought them gifts.

Traditional Nuremberg angel

Nutcracker decoration

Christmas star

Silent Night
Carols were very popular. The German carol *Stille Nacht* ('Silent Night') was composed at the same time that Hoffmann was writing.

Children acted in nativity plays, dressing in special costumes.

Christmas tree
The tree was the focal point of the Christmas season. Trees were hung with apples and nuts painted silver and gold, wooden figures, and sugarplums. Candles were also lit on the tree. The traditional hanging figures are still made today.

Christmas fairs

Many German cities held a Christ child's market. The most famous was in Nuremberg, where Marie and Fritz lived. People bought fir trees, decorations, toys, and spice cakes from stalls. The air was filled with the smell of pine needles, roasted chestnuts, and spiced wine.

A Christ child's market is still held in Nuremberg.

Magical Martinmas

The feast of St. Martin, or Martinmas, was a magical time when children lit pretty Chinese lanterns and carried them in processions. In the story, lights of all kinds are symbols of magic and discovery.

Children with Martinmas lanterns

Christmas cracker

From the 18th century, nutcrackers became popular Christmas gifts. Children could play with them; adults could use them.

CHRISTMAS TREATS

Germany is famous for its festive treats of spiced cookies and cakes, such as stollen, a rich fruit and almond cake. Another favorite is spicy gingerbread, which the Stahlbaum children eat on Christmas Eve.

Traditional stollen cake

Stars and hearts are still favorite cookie shapes at Christmas.

Pfeffernusse traditional spicy nut cookies

Christmas wreath with sugarplums

A delicious iced gingerbread tree

Traditional wooden candleholders

The special Christmas Star of Bethlehem

Gold star

In the Christmas story, the three wise men follow a star, which leads them to the baby Jesus. In *The Nutcracker* Hoffmann shows how, if you follow the stars, your dreams can come true.

Three wise men

German children loved "starsinging." They dressed up as the three kings and carried a star in a procession. They sang carols as they walked.

GERMAN TOYS

M arie and Fritz were lucky to be living in Nuremberg in the early 19th century. Germany's toys were the best in Europe. Parents could buy all kinds of toys, including traditional wooden ones, tin soldiers, jumping jacks, and dolls dressed in beautiful clothes. The most sophisticated toys were mechanical figures and objects, known as "automata." Some were as complex as Drosselmeier's amazing clockwork castle. Automata were designed to appeal more to adults than children.

Toy centers

This map shows the major areas of toy production in Germany in the 1800s.

Erzgebirge and Sonneberg are still famous for toys – and nutcrackers!

Clockwork toys, like this racing car, came from Nuremberg and southwest Germany.

Forested areas such as Grodnertal were famous for producing wooden dolls.

Gretel has a bisque (porcelain) face.

DAINTY DOLLS

Dolls were made from wood, pâpier-maché or cloth, or a combination of these materials.

Eva has jointed limbs

Tortoise-shell comb is painted

Eva was made in 1810. Her dress is a traditional chintz.

Chic and cheerful

Fashionably dressed French dolls and their accessories were exported to Germany and the United States.

In the story, Fritz's lions and tigers come alive.

Tin men in uniform

From about 1750, tin soldiers were made in Germany and Switzerland. The standard sizes were set in Nuremberg: 1.25 in (3.5 cm) for foot soldiers and 1.75 in (4 cm) for mounted cavalrymen. During the Napoleonic Wars children collected toy armies modelled on the real armies.

Careful carving

In the story, Fritz gets figures for his Noah's ark. Painted wooden arks were educational and fun, so they were very popular. This early 19th-century ark is from Sonneberg.

By the mid-19th century, porcelain dolls were popular in Germany. Gretel was made by the famous German firm, Simon and Halbig. She wears German folk costume.

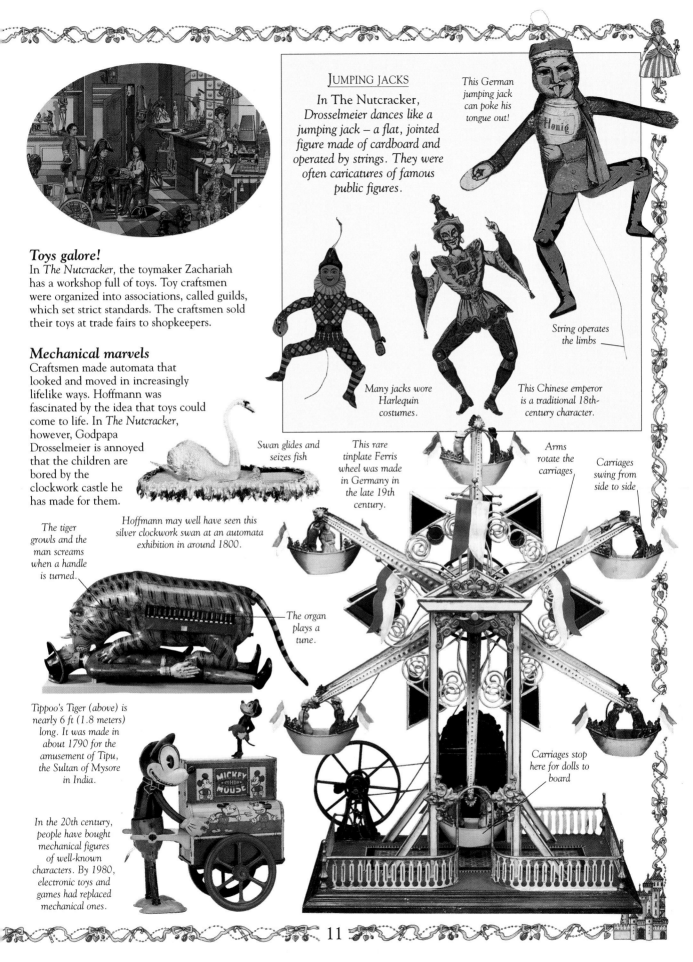

Toys galore!

In *The Nutcracker*, the toymaker Zachariah has a workshop full of toys. Toy craftsmen were organized into associations, called guilds, which set strict standards. The craftsmen sold their toys at trade fairs to shopkeepers.

Mechanical marvels

Craftsmen made automata that looked and moved in increasingly lifelike ways. Hoffmann was fascinated by the idea that toys could come to life. In *The Nutcracker*, however, Godpapa Drosselmeier is annoyed that the children are bored by the clockwork castle he has made for them.

Swan glides and seizes fish

Hoffmann may well have seen this silver clockwork swan at an automata exhibition in around 1800.

The tiger growls and the man screams when a handle is turned.

Tippoo's Tiger (above) is nearly 6 ft (1.8 meters) long. It was made in about 1790 for the amusement of Tipu, the Sultan of Mysore in India.

In the 20th century, people have bought mechanical figures of well-known characters. By 1980, electronic toys and games had replaced mechanical ones.

JUMPING JACKS

In The Nutcracker, Drosselmeier dances like a jumping jack – a flat, jointed figure made of cardboard and operated by strings. They were often caricatures of famous public figures.

This German jumping jack can poke his tongue out!

Honig

String operates the limbs

Many jacks wore Harlequin costumes.

This Chinese emperor is a traditional 18th-century character.

This rare tinplate Ferris wheel was made in Germany in the late 19th century.

Arms rotate the carriages

Carriages swing from side to side

The organ plays a tune.

Carriages stop here for dolls to board

Godpapa would take off his wig, put on his apron, and set to work.

Wig wearing
In early 19th-century Europe, wealthy men wore wigs both to conceal baldness and to show their high social status. The wigs were made of human hair or horsehair.

Like clockwork
Germany had produced brilliant clock- and watchmakers since medieval times. Nuremberg was particularly famous for this and for its clockwork toys.

Chapter one

CHRISTMAS EVE

IT WAS CHRISTMAS EVE and Fritz and Marie Stahlbaum had been banned from the drawing room all day. The children sat waiting in the parlor, very excited and trying to be patient. As the evening shadows deepened eerily around them, Fritz told Marie, who was only seven, a secret. Since early morning he had heard strange noises coming from behind the doors. Rattlings and rustlings, tinkerings and hammerings.

"What's more," whispered Fritz mysteriously, "I've seen a strange little man in black creeping around the house, carrying a big box."

"Godpapa!" gasped Marie. "I wonder what he's brought us?"

Godpapa Drosselmeier always gave them the most clever and pretty toys. He wasn't pretty himself, though. He was small and wiry and wrinkled, with a black patch over his right eye. He was bald, too, and wore a fine wig on top of his head. But he was very clever. So clever that he knew everything about clocks and watches.

Whenever one of Dr. Stahlbaum's clocks had stopped working, Drosselmeier came to the rescue. He would take off his wig and yellow jacket, put on his apron, and set to work with his sharp little instruments. Soon, the clock would be whirring happily again.

Best of all was at Christmas, when he would make something wonderfully ingenious for the Stahlbaum family. This year, Marie thought it might be the magical lake her godfather had once told her about, where a little girl fed shortbread to graceful swans. Fritz was sure the gift would be a huge fortress full of fighting soldiers.

The children talked in hushed voices about their presents. Fritz wanted a fox for his ark and some hussars for his toy army. Marie hoped for a new doll. Suddenly they heard a *Ting-a-ling-a-ling!* Mama was ringing a little silver bell. The drawing room doors flew open and a brilliant light came flooding out.

Imagine the magical sight that met their eyes! There stood the Christmas tree, decorated with gold and silver apples and sugar-plums, and glittering with little candles. The whole room sparkled!

The curtain drew back and there stood a magnificent castle.

Chapter two

THE PRESENTS

"OH, HOW LOVELY!" sighed Marie as she gazed in wonder at the tree. Fritz started jumping up and down with excitement.

"Go on," said Mama, smiling, "find out what the Christ child has brought for you good children!"

The children ran here, there, and everywhere.

Marie discovered the most beautiful dolls, all sorts of picture books, and a pretty silk dress with colored ribbons hanging from one of the branches. Fritz found not only a fox but a whole squadron of hussars, too. They wore red and gold uniforms with real silver swords, and they were mounted on fine white horses.

The children calmed down a little and began to look at the picture books. Marie was enchanted with what she saw. There were strange flowers, lively portraits of people from all over the world, children laughing and playing. They looked so real!

Soon their parents called them to a table where something was hidden behind a green curtain. It was Godpapa's special present.

The curtain drew back and there stood a magnificent castle. It had sparkling windows and golden towers with bells that chimed. Doors and windows opened to reveal little ladies and gentlemen in long robes and plumed hats. They walked up and down inside the rooms of the castle, while tiny children in silk and velvet gowns danced to the bells and a man in a green cloak popped out his head. Even a small model of Godpapa Drosselmeier came to the castle doors. He was no bigger than your thumb.

"Let me go inside," begged Fritz.

"I'm afraid that's quite impossible, young man," said the real Drosselmeier, shaking his head.

"Then make them do something different," grumbled Fritz.

When Drosselmeier explained that the figures were part of a clockwork and couldn't do anything different, Fritz looked very disappointed. He thought they weren't half as good as his soldiers, which he could command as he pleased. So he wandered off to play with his squadron of hussars, and soon had them charging around in fierce combat. Even Marie, who was also bored but was too kind and gentle to show it, slipped quietly away. Drosselmeier was rather offended until Mrs. Stahlbaum came to the rescue and asked him to show her how everything worked.

Marie was nibbling a delicious gingerbread man when she noticed something she hadn't seen before. Sitting quietly under the Christmas tree was an odd little gentleman in a hussar's jacket.

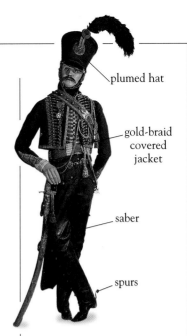

plumed hat

gold-braid covered jacket

saber

spurs

Hussars
A hussar was a soldier in a light cavalry regiment. Hussars were renowned for their elegant uniforms and beautiful horses. They often did reconnaissance work – information gathering.

Castles in the air
In the 19th century the German aristocracy would indulge their taste for the romantic and the fantastic. They built fabulous castles like Neuschwanstein in southern Germany, above. Toymakers responded by making miniature castles in amazing detail.

Chapter three

MARIE'S PET

The little man opened his mouth wider and wider, showing off his sharp, white teeth.

MARIE FELL HEAD OVER HEELS in love with this wonderful little man. Maybe his body was too long, his legs too thin and his head too large. Maybe his short cloak, which looked like wood, did seem rather silly and his hat was like a miner's. Maybe he did look like Godpapa Drosselmeier.

But that pretty purple jacket covered in braid and those splendid little boots made up for everything. Besides, as Marie stared at him, she realized what a sweet nature he had. His green eyes (which stuck out a little too far) glowed with kindness. His chin, with its white, cotton beard, showed off the smile on his bright, red lips.

"Papa," asked Marie, "who's this darling man?"

"He belongs to all of you," said her father. "You, Fritz, and your sister Louise. He's going to crack nuts for you."

Dr. Stahlbaum picked up the little man and lifted his wooden cloak. At once he opened his mouth wider and wider, showing off his sharp, white teeth. Marie put a nut inside his mouth and he bit it in two with a loud CRACK!

Dr. Stahlbaum explained that he came from the Nutcracker family and was practicing the trade of his ancestors.

"And since Marie likes him so much," he added, "I'm putting him in her special care."

Marie scooped the nutcracker up in her arms and made him crack some more nuts. She was careful to choose the smallest, so he didn't have to open his mouth too wide. But Fritz was tired of drilling his soldiers, so he demanded a try. Laughing at the funny little fellow, Fritz made sure Nutcracker cracked the biggest and hardest nuts. He was doing just that when there was a terrible *SNACK-SNACK!* Three of Nutcracker's teeth fell out and his jaw flopped open.

"Poor, darling Nutcracker!" cried Marie, pulling him away.

"What good is he now?" said Fritz. "I'll soon lick him into shape!"

"No," answered Marie angrily, "you're cruel! You beat your horses and shoot your men."

"He's as much mine as yours!" shouted Fritz. "Hand him over!"

Marie burst into tears and wrapped Nutcracker carefully in her handkerchief. Papa heard the quarrel and spoke sternly, "Fritz, you should be ashamed of forcing an injured soldier into service like that!"

Marie took her wounded little man, tied a white ribbon around his broken jaw, and rocked him in her arms while she read her books.

Marie rocked him in her arms.

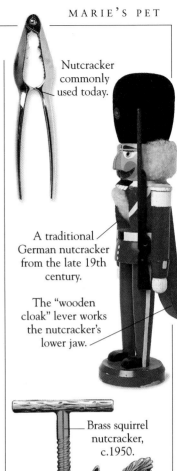

Nutcracker commonly used today.

A traditional German nutcracker from the late 19th century.

The "wooden cloak" lever works the nutcracker's lower jaw.

Brass squirrel nutcracker, c.1950.

Completely nuts!
Nutcrackers have been used in Europe for over 600 years. Over the centuries many inventive designs have been developed, though some creations were more fun than practical!

Yuletide uniforms
Traditional wooden nutcrackers, carved in the form of military figures, have been made as Christmas gifts in southeast Germany since the late 17th century.

18th-century German doll.

Dainty doll
German dolls were beautifully crafted. They were often sold unclothed and their exquisite clothes and accessories were made by their owners' mothers or professional dolls' dressmakers.

At the mention of Drosselmeier, Nutcracker made a horrid, ugly face.

Chapter four

WONDERFUL EVENTS

IN THE SITTING ROOM, against the left wall, was a tall glass cabinet where the Stahlbaums displayed the children's Christmas books and toys. On the top shelf were Godpapa Drosselmeier's works of art, beneath them the picture books, below that Fritz's soldiers and, on the lowest shelf, Marie's dolls.

One called Miss Gertrude was sitting there now, on a floral sofa in an elegant room with a lovely white bed, next to Marie's new doll, whose name was Miss Clara.

It was getting very late, close to midnight in fact, and Drosselmeier had gone home hours ago. But although it was long past their bedtime, the children's eyes were still fixed on the cabinet.

Fritz yawned, "My hussars must be exhausted, but none of them dares fall asleep while I'm watching."

He saluted them sleepily and went to bed. Marie begged her mother to be allowed to stay up a little longer. She was such a good little girl that her mother agreed. She put out all the candles, leaving only a lamp burning softly from the ceiling, and kissed her daughter goodnight.

When Marie was sure she was alone, she set to work. She laid Nutcracker gently on the table and, unwrapping the handkerchief, started examining his wounds.

He looked terribly pale, but he was still smiling bravely – though a little sadly.

"Darling Nutcracker," whispered Marie, " I'll nurse you back to health and make you happy again; and Godpapa Drosselmeier will fix your teeth."

At the mention of Drosselmeier something amazing happened. Nutcracker made a horrid, ugly face and a green glint sparked from his eyes.

Marie was terrified, until she looked at Nutcracker again

"You're not going to sleep next to nasty Miss Clara," Marie added coldly.

and saw him smiling back at her.

She decided that the sudden change in his appearance must have been caused by the flickering lamplight. Relieved, Marie picked Nutcracker up, and knelt down by the cabinet to address Miss Clara.

"I want to ask a favor. Will you give up your bed for my poor Nutcracker?" But Miss Clara didn't answer and looked back so scornfully that Marie shrugged.

"Then I won't be polite either," she said. Pulling the bed forward, she laid Nutcracker down. She wrapped another ribbon around his shoulder and pulled the bedclothes up to his nose.

"You're not going to sleep next to nasty Miss Clara," Marie added coldly, before moving the bed to the next shelf, near Fritz's troops, and closing the cabinet door.

19

Just as the door shut, Marie heard a soft rustling all around
her. The clock on the wall whirred louder and louder.
It was ready to strike midnight. Marie suddenly saw that
the golden owl on the top had spread its wings.
Then the clock rang out with these strange words:
   "Bells Chime. Now it's time …
In midnight's gloom, sing Mouse King's doom!"
   When she looked at the clock again,
Godpapa Drosselmeier was sitting on
the clock instead of the owl!
   "Don't scare me, naughty Godpapa!"
she cried.
   But now the room was filled with
wild squeaking and the tramp of
thousands of little feet behind the
skirting boards. Tiny lights began to
glimmer through the cracks. Only
they weren't lights. They were
eyes. Thousands
of glittering eyes!
   Suddenly the
room filled with
mice, galloping
everywhere and forming into
troops like Fritz's soldiers.
   Unlike many children Marie
wasn't afraid of mice, so she found
it all very funny. But then she heard
a cry that froze her blood. Sand and
broken stones burst up at her feet,
and out of the floor rose an
enormous mouse with seven heads.
   On each head was
a golden crown.

*Out of the floor
rose an enormous
mouse.*

He hissed horribly and his army advanced
on the cabinet.

As Marie stepped back in terror, her elbow
shattered a pane of glass in the cabinet. She felt
a sharp pain in her arm, but her fear
suddenly subsided. The squeaking had
stopped. Marie thought she'd scared
the mice back into their holes.

When everything was quiet Marie
heard urgent whispering from
inside the cabinet.

*"The battle's tonight. Left, right!
Now we are to march and fight!"*
Behind the glass doors
glowed a brilliant light.
The toys were coming to
life. Nutcracker himself
sprang out of bed and
drew his sword.

"Who'll fight beside me?"
he cried valiantly.

Then he jumped from the
second shelf and would have
broken his legs if Miss Clara hadn't
caught him in her arms.

"My Lord," she wept, "stay with me!
Let your subjects do the fighting!"

But Nutcracker kicked so hard she let
him go. Then she offered him her sash
for good luck. Although he thanked her
graciously, the loyal Nutcracker took Marie's
ribbon instead. He kissed it and jumped to
the floor where the mouse army was
waiting, led by their terrible
seven-headed king.

Chapter five

THE BATTLE

"SOUND THE ADVANCE, faithful drummer!" cried Nutcracker, and the drumroll made the glass cabinet rattle furiously. Then, as Marie watched, there was a strange clattering inside. All the lids on the boxes of Fritz's toy soldiers suddenly burst open and out sprang the little army. The soldiers jumped down to the bottom shelf and formed up neatly as Nutcracker rushed boldly along their ranks.

"Why don't any of you blasted trumpeters sound the call!?" shouted Nutcracker angrily. He turned to the commander, who was looking very pale.

"General, you're brave and experienced," Nutcracker said solemnly, "and we need to master the situation quickly. Take command of the cavalry and artillery and do your duty!"

The General whistled louder than a hundred trumpets, and Marie heard a tramping and neighing from the cupboard.

The regiment of hussars, glittering in their brand new coats, came trooping out to face the mice. Their band played and their banners waved as they marched past Nutcracker.

Next, Fritz's artillery swung into action, drawing up on the floor in front of the waiting cavalry. *Boom, boom!* went the guns, as a shower of sugarplums shot from the cannons, and plastered the mouse battalions in white powder. But the heavy guns did the most damage from their position on top of Mama's footstool. *Poom, poom, poom!* they blazed, mowing down the mice in a murderous barrage of gingernuts.

Everyone fought bravely, of course. The advancing mouse battalions kept bringing up more reserves. They even captured a few guns, so it was unclear which side was winning for a long time. Marie could hardly see anything through the smoke and sugar dust. The noise of the cannon blasts was deafening, and the skillful mice peppered the hussars with little balls of silver shot. The evil-smelling shot made horrid, dark spots on the hussar's uniforms, or it whizzed and whistled past to smash into the glass cabinet.

"To die so young," wailed Miss Clara, "and the prettiest doll in all the world!" She clung to Gertrude, who sobbed bitterly, "Am I to be shot in my own drawing room after preserving myself so carefully all these years?"

infantry drum

cavalry trumpet

Musical messages
On 19th-century battlefields generals ordered drummers and trumpeters to sound different tunes as signals for action. The infantry (foot soldiers) charged first. The mounted cavalry followed. The artillery fired the cannons.

A shower of sugar-plums shot from the cannons.

18th-century Meissen porcelain figurine

Harlequin

The clownlike Harlequin is one of a group of stock characters from 17th-century Italian plays known as commedia dell'arte.

Above the fierce din came Nutcracker's powerful voice, issuing orders and shouting encouragement as he strode bravely back and forth in the thick of battle. However, some of the troops were suffering so much that they suddenly wheeled around and retreated to their quarters. This exposed the footstool which, under attack from a very ugly bunch of mice, fell into enemy hands.

Nutcracker was so disconcerted that he ordered his right wing to retreat, threatening disaster for the whole army. But no – look there! The left wing was still holding up gallantly. Then reinforcements came from an elite battalion of motto figures, made up of wonderfully uniformed harlequins, darling cupids, monkeys, lions, tigers, and unicorns. Two Chinese emperors commanded them to advance and form a square. How bravely they fought!

They would have won the battle, but for a vicious mouse captain.

Reinforcements came from an elite battalion of motto figures.

motto inside cookie

Eat your words

Wise sayings and wishes hidden inside ornaments were popular in Europe, especially for festive occasions. The Chinese still make traditional fortune cookies with rice-paper messages inside them.

He bit off one of the Chinese emperor's heads. The victim's fall knocked over a tiger and a unicorn and made a gap through which the mice rushed. The whole battalion was bitten to death. The bloodthirsty mice from that squadron bit off more than they could chew, though, for every time one of them gnawed through the neck of a motto figure, the mouse choked to death on the piece of paper inside. *"Don't let your eyes be bigger than your stomach!"* one motto read.

During the hottest part of the battle, mouse cavalry had been emerging from under the chest of drawers and now, squeaking horribly, they charged the left wing. Once the retreat had started, there was no stopping it. Nutcracker was pushed back and soon found himself pressed right up against the cupboard, with hardly a man left.

"Generals, drummers, where have you all gone?" he cried desperately. "Bring up the reserves!"

A small contingent of gingerbread men did advance, but they fought so clumsily that the enemy soon bit off their legs.

Nutcracker was in terrible danger. He tried to leap into the cabinet, but his legs were too short. And since Gertrude and Miss Clara had fainted, they couldn't help him.

"A horse, a horse, my kingdom for a horse!" cried Nutcracker, as the King of Mice came charging at him, squeaking from all seven throats.

"Oh, my poor Nutcracker!" gasped Marie. She tore off her shoe and threw it straight at the King.

Instantly everything vanished. Marie felt her arm stinging again, and she fainted to the floor.

Marie tore off her shoe and threw it straight at the Mouse King.

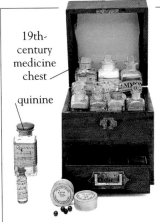

19th-century medicine chest

quinine

Wound fever
On the battlefield, disinfectant was used to clean wounds. Quinine was given to lower a fever, but many soldiers still died of "wound fever" when their injuries became infected.

Chapter six

THE INVALID

W HEN MARIE WOKE UP SHE WAS IN BED and the sun was streaming through the windows. The first thing she noticed was the frost patterns on the window panes. She turned her head and saw a man sitting by her bed. Then she recognized him – it was Dr. Wendelstern. Mama stood beside him, looking anxious.

"Oh, Mama," whispered Marie, "have all the mice gone?"

Dr. Wendelstern looked at Marie's mother and raised his eyebrows.

"What are you talking about?" answered her mother, "you were playing so late last night you must have fallen asleep against the cabinet, broken the glass and cut your arm. I found you on the floor surrounded by broken toys, gingerbread men, and Fritz's soldiers.

Dr. Wendelstern raised his eyebrows.

Nutcracker was lying on your injured arm, and your shoe was on the floor nearby."

"But, Mama," protested Marie, "there was a terrible battle, and the mice nearly took Nutcracker prisoner!"

At this, Marie's father came in and she heard him whispering to Dr. Wendelstern about "wound fever."

Marie had to stay in bed for several days after that, although she didn't feel ill at all. She knew that Nutcracker was safe, for she could clearly remember that he had thanked her. Strangely, he had added, "But dearest lady, you have the power to do even more for me."

Marie could not think what on earth this could be.

One day Mama had just finished telling her a story when Godpapa Drosselmeier came by to check how the invalid was getting along. Marie looked at him crossly and cried, "Godpapa, why didn't you help Nutcracker last night?"

Drosselmeier made an extraordinary face and, jerking his arms up and down like a jumping jack, started to snarl, "*Click, clack, snickety snack, clocks whirr, dolls crack!*"

Fritz, who had just come in, burst out laughing; but Mama looked gravely at Drosselmeier and asked, "What can you mean by this behavior?"

"Haven't you heard my watchmaker's song?" smiled Drosselmeier. "Don't be cross with me, Marie. Look, here's something that will please you."

Drosselmeier reached into his pocket and took out – Nutcracker! His teeth were back and his jaw was fixed.

"But he's still very ugly," said Drosselmeier. "If you like I'll tell you why. It's because of Princess Pirlipat, the witch Mouserink, and the clever clockmaker."

"Where's Nutcracker's sword?" asked Fritz suddenly.

"Don't interrupt, boy!" snapped Drosselmeier. "He'll just have to find another sword for himself. Now, Marie, would you like to hear the story of Pirlipat?"

"Yes please!" cried Marie.

And Drosselmeier began his story like this.

Drosselmeier jerked up and down like a jumping jack

silver, double-ended medicine cup

silver medicine spoon

Childhood suffering
Children, rich and poor, often fell victim to fatal diseases such as tuberculosis. Medical advice was frequently useless. Parents took their need to watch over their children very seriously.

The king danced on one leg from joy.

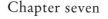

Chapter seven

THE STORY OF PIRLIPAT

Mad Max
Maximilian I was King of Bavaria in Hoffmann's time. The writer's eccentric royal characters may have been inspired by the alleged madness in the Bavarian royal family at that time.

satin drapes

Cradle comfort
The Swan Cradle provided a luxurious bed for the baby of a wealthy German family around 1800. It is made of gold-embossed mahogany.

"PIRLIPAT'S PARENTS were the king and queen, which made Pirlipat a princess," Godpapa Drosselmeier began. "She was born the prettiest princess you have ever seen. Her little face looked as though it was made of the finest pink and white silk. Her eyes were a sparkling blue, and her hair looked like spun gold. What is more, she was born with two rows of pearly white teeth, which she immediately used to bite the Lord Chancellor's hand. Everybody knew she was very intelligent indeed!

"Pirlipat was so lovely that the king, all the ministers of state, the generals, and the presidents, danced around her cradle on one leg from joy.

"All were happy, except that the queen worried terribly about her little daughter, and had her cradle carefully guarded. Apart from the guards at the nursery door and the two chief nurses by the crib, there were always six other nurses by the cradle at night. And what nobody could understand was why each nurse had a cat on her lap, which she stroked continuously to make sure that it purred all night long. You couldn't possibly know the reason for this, so I'll tell you.

"Before Pirlipat was born, there was a wonderful party at the king and queen's palace.

Nobody could
understand why each
nurse had a cat
on her lap.

Wiener

Regensburger
Knackwurst

Rotkohl

Greasy grub
*Puddings were savory, made
out of blood, fat, and spices
like black pudding today.
Germany has always been
famous for producing some
of the best sausages in the
world, like Frankfurters and
Bratwurst.*

The king had decided to show just how rich he was by throwing
a huge pudding and sausage banquet. He ordered the Chancellor
of the Exchequer to bring out the Great Golden Sausage Kettle and
the silver casserole dishes. Then the king called the queen to his
side and said sweetly, "Darling, you know how much I like sausages!"
The queen knew that this meant she should do the cooking.

Chafing dish used for keeping food warm.

fragrant sandalwood

Old flames

Before the 20th century, Europeans cooked food in pots over a fire or roasted it on spits (skewers). In wealthy households the maids burned sandalwood for its spicy smell, which masked unpleasant cooking odors.

Mouserink's uncles and aunts all demanded some delicious fat.

"A huge fire of sandalwood was lit in the royal kitchens, the queen put on her damask apron, and the most delicious smell of sausage, bacon, and spicy pudding soon wafted through the palace.

"Then the time arrived for the bacon to be cut into little squares and browned on silver spits. The ladies-in-waiting departed and left the queen all on her own.

"But just as the bacon started to brown, the queen heard a low whispering in the kitchen:

'Oh, I want a bit of that tasty bacon, too! Please give me some, sister,' said a small, plaintive voice. 'I'm a queen like you.'

"The queen knew who was speaking. It was Dame Mouserink, who had lived in the palace for many years. She claimed to be related to the royal family and was the Queen of Mousalia herself. She lived, with a big family, under the kitchen hearth.

"Though the queen would never accept that Mouserink was related to her, she was kind-hearted and it was a festive occasion. So she decided to give Mouserink a little of the bacon to eat. Dame Mouserink scurried from the hearth, as fast as she could, and held up her little paws.

The queen handed her slice after slice of the tasty crisp bacon.

"Now something terrible happened. Out jumped Dame Mouserink's uncles, aunts, cousins and her seven lazy sons, too. In a chorus of squeaks and squeals they all demanded a share of the bacon. The poor queen was too frightened to refuse, so she fed them all.

"Fortunately for her, the Mistress of the Robes soon came in and shooed them all away. But when the poor queen looked at the bacon, she gasped. It was nearly all gone! In despair, she summoned the court mathematician. With some very complicated calculations he was just able to divide the remaining bacon among the royal sausages.

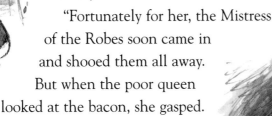
The queen summoned the court mathematician.

Empress Josephine of France with her ladies-in-waiting

Mistress of the Robes
Even today a queen has a Mistress of the Robes, one of her ladies-in-waiting, to take care of her splendid dresses. The Mistress of the Robes is herself a member of the aristocracy.

"Not enough bacon, not enough bacon!" the king whimpered.

"Upstairs in the royal dining rooms the kettledrums crashed, the trumpets sounded, and all the great princes arrived in their silver coaches for the feast. In the Great Banqueting Hall, acrobats tumbled, jesters juggled, and players masqueraded magnificently.

"The king sat at the head of the table with his crown on his head and a golden scepter in his hand. But when the sausages and puddings were handed around the king turned pale, fell back in his chair, and groaned. The tumbling, the juggling, the singing and the laughter stopped. All eyes were on the king. The court physician rushed up and revived His Majesty with some powerful smelling salts. He whimpered, very faintly, 'Not enough bacon, not enough bacon!'

"At this the queen threw herself at his feet.

'Oh my poor darling,' she sobbed, 'how you are suffering! But the culprits are at your feet. It was Dame Mouserink and her family who ate your bacon ...'

"The poor queen then fainted.

"The king jumped up angrily and decided to take a terrible revenge on Dame Mouserink and her family. He summoned the court clockmaker, whose name was just the same as mine: Christian Elias Drosselmeier. Drosselmeier was ordered to drive Mouserink and all her relations from the palace forever.

"So Drosselmeier set to work and invented amazing little traps. He put pieces of browned bacon inside them and placed the traps, carefully, outside Dame Mouserink's dwelling.

32

"The smell of the bacon was much too good to resist. So Dame Mouserink's seven sons and most of her relations died horribly in the palace kitchens.

"But Dame Mouserink's heart burned with anger and hatred. Before she and her diminished retinue left the palace, she vowed she would have revenge on the king. The next day, when the queen was in the kitchen cooking the king a mutton stew, Dame Mouserink suddenly popped up in front of her.

'Be careful,' she hissed, 'or one day the Queen of Mice will bite your little princess in two!'

"The queen was so frightened that she dropped the stew in the fire and ruined the poor king's dinner. She then sought advice from the court astrologer.

He told her that only the famous feline family of Cat Purr could keep Mouserink away."

Drosselmeier invented amazing little traps.

steel drowning chamber

lever

trap door

mouse

Steel German mousetrap

Mouse in the house

Wooden floorboards used to have plenty of holes for mice to get through. Even royal palaces were overrun by mice. Cats and traps were used everywhere. Often there were as many as 30 cats in a royal household.

33

Chapter eight

DROSSELMEIER CONTINUES

Horror of horrors! What had Pirlipat turned into?

Shock and horror
Moral tales like The Nutcracker *were popular in the 19th century. They often combined humour with horror. Carlo Collodi's tale of* Pinocchio, *is an example.*

"SO NOW YOU KNOW WHY Pirlipat's nursery was full of cats," said Godpapa Drosselmeier. Marie looked at him and asked, "Was it really you who invented mousetraps?"

Drosselmeier smiled mysteriously and continued his story.

"One dark night, soon after Pirlipat was born," he whispered, "one of her head nurses was woken from a very deep sleep. Everything was quiet. There was not a purr to be heard. But imagine the nurse's shock when she saw, in Pirlipat's cradle, an enormous mouse with its head near the Princess's face!

"Her screams woke all the other nurses and the cats, who chased Dame Mouserink off through a hole in the wall. Then Pirlipat started crying. Thank goodness – she was still alive! The nurses looked in her cradle – horror of horrors! What had Pirlipat turned into? Her pretty face was now a bloated head wobbling on top of a horrid, crumpled body. Her lovely blue eyes were now ghastly green orbs staring back above a mouth that stretched from ear to ear.

"When her parents saw Pirlipat, the queen sobbed inconsolably. The king banged his head against the palace walls. But instead of knocking some sense into him and making him see that he should have forgiven the greedy mice, the king blamed the clockmaker.

"His Majesty issued an edict saying that if Drosselmeier didn't restore Princess Pirlipat within four weeks the court executioner would chop off his head.

"Drosselmeier didn't have much time. He took Princess Pirlipat carefully to pieces, unscrewing her hands and feet and examining her insides. But when he had finished and put her back together, he shook his head, dejectedly, and gave up.

"Wednesday of the fourth week arrived.

'Drosselmeier,' shouted the king angrily, 'restore Pirlipat or prepare to die!'

"The clockmaker started weeping. Little Pirlipat sat staring at him, a large nut in her mouth. Through his tears Drosselmeier looked at the ugly child. He realized that ever since her transformation the only thing that stopped her from crying was when a nurse gave her a nut to crack.

'Oh eternal interdependence of things!' cried Drosselmeier, and he immediately asked to see his old friend the court astrologer.

"They hugged each other, then locked themselves away for three days and nights to consult the stars. They pored over many mysterious books, peered through a telescope, and drew up the Princess's horoscope.

At last, joy of joys, they found the solution.

chart

Star-struck
For centuries, astrologers have used horoscope charts to study the position of the stars at a person's birth to predict their future.

They peered through a telescope.

They traveled for fifteen long years.

pecan

walnut

Cracking the problem
The image of cracking a nut implies that Pirlipat can only become a person when someone has proved that they truly love her. The kernel of truth lies beneath the shell of appearances.

"At dinner on Saturday Drosselmeier told the king what he had discovered. The one thing that could lift the spell cast upon Pirlipat was if she ate the kernel of the great nut Crackatook.

"Crackatook's shell was so hard that a forty-eight pound cannon couldn't smash it. Crackatook had to be cracked, in front of the princess, by a man who'd never shaven and never worn any boots. What's more, the man had to hand her the kernel with his eyes shut and take seven steps backwards without tripping up.

"When he heard the news the king hugged Drosselmeier.

'Well then, my friend,' he smiled, 'what are you waiting for?'

"But now the clockmaker trembled and stammered out that he had not yet found the great nut Crackatook, or the man to crack it.

'What?!' screamed His Majesty. 'Then off with your head!'

"It was lucky for Drosselmeier that the king ate a particularly good dinner that evening, and for once he listened to the queen's advice.

Feeling sorry for the clockmaker, she persuaded the king to let Drosselmeier search for the nut. Meanwhile, she suggested, His Majesty should advertise in the local and foreign newspapers and gazettes for the right man to crack Crackatook.

"Before the king could change his mind, Drosselmeier and the astrologer set off, vowing not to return until they had found the nut.

"The companions traveled for fifteen long years. They spent two years at the court of the King of Dates. They then searched the realm of the King of Almonds – but were soon expelled from there. They even asked at the Natural History Society in Squirreltown. But they couldn't find the great Crackatook anywhere.

"At last they sat down in the middle of a great forest in Asia to study their map. They were brewing jasmine tea when Drosselmeier had a sudden desire to see his hometown of Nuremberg.

'Nuremberg, oh Nuremberg, my beautiful town,' he sighed sadly, 'your houses have windows both upstairs and down.'

"The astrologer felt bitterly sorry that his friend was homesick and they both burst into tears. Their loud sobs startled all the radiant birds and roaring beasts who lived in the vast, shady forest.

'Why not Nuremberg?' cried the astrologer suddenly, wiping his eyes. 'Let's look there!'

'Why not indeed?' said Drosselmeier."

Early advertising
In the 18th and 19th centuries, newspapers were one of the few media available for advertising products, services, and job vacancies.

"Oh Nuremberg, my beautiful town," he sighed sadly.

Nuremberg
The winding streets and old buildings of Nuremberg's center give the city a fairy-tale atmosphere.

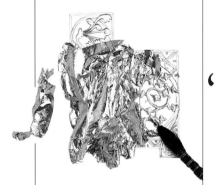

Golden oldies
The nut Crackatook has been gilded, or painted gold. Gilders often worked closely with carpenters, covering their finely wrought objects with gold. Some craftsmen were experts in both trades.

Chinese lettering
19th-century scholars might have known how to read Chinese. Chinese words read from top to bottom - this means "Nutcracker."

堅
果
鉗

The toymaker pulled a golden nut out of a cardboard box.

Chapter nine

CRACKATOOK

"WHEN THEY REACHED Nuremberg, Drosselmeier suggested that they visit his cousin, Zachariah, who was a toymaker, a doll-carver, and a master gilder. They told Zachariah all about Princess Pirlipat, evil Mouserink, the Great Nut Crackatook, and their adventures.

"As the toymaker listened he grew more and more excited, until he suddenly threw his wig in the air, and shouted, 'But cousin, your troubles are over. Crackatook is *here*!'

"The toymaker explained that one Christmas, some years ago, a stranger had arrived at his toy shop with a bag of nuts for sale. The man had been attacked by the local nut sellers, and his bag was run over by a heavy cart which smashed all the nuts except one. The stranger sold him this unusual nut for a gold coin dated 1796.

"The toymaker then pulled a golden nut out of a cardboard box. The astrologer carefully scraped away the gold and imagine the joyful surprise when there on the side of the nut, in Chinese letters, they saw the word CRACKATOOK. But their excitement was much greater when, that night, the astrologer said, 'Good luck always comes in pairs. We've not only found the great nut, but, perhaps, the man to crack it. Here he is – Zachariah's son!'

"Zachariah's son was very handsome and had never shaven or worn any boots. He stood in the shop wearing a fine red coat, a splendid pigtail, and a sword by his side. Dressed like this he spent his time cracking nuts for the young ladies, who called him 'the handsome nutcracker.'

'Quick!' said the astrologer. 'I'm going to draw his horoscope.'

"The next morning the astrologer walked into the toymaker's kitchen waving a horoscope chart triumphantly and cried, 'It *is* him! And I've found out something else. We must let several other young men attempt to crack Crackatook before Nutcracker. I predict that when they fail, the king will promise the throne and Pirlipat's hand in marriage to the man who breaks the nut.'

"At this, the toymaker's son was delighted. He let his uncle make him an especially strong pigtail made of wood, which was then tied to his jaw. For practice, he spent the rest of the day cracking the hardest peach stones he could find, and walking backward while wearing a blindfold.

Drosselmeier made him an especially strong pigtail.

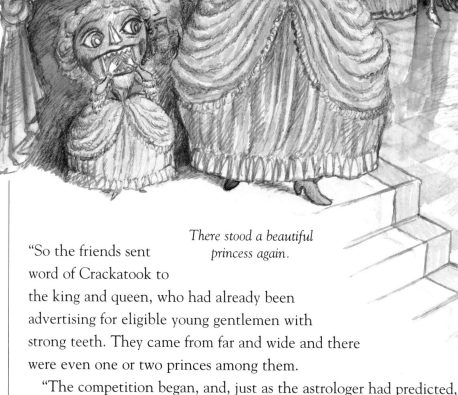

The power of love
The themes of love and
magical transformation
appear in fairy tales published
before Hoffmann was born.
One example is Mme. de
Beaumont's Beauty and the
Beast, written in 1756.

Beauty and the Beast
Beauty is held prisoner by a
sad, beastlike man. He loves
her, and she grows to love
him. He frees her and almost
dies of a broken heart but she
returns to him. Her love
breaks the evil spell – he
turns back into a fine prince!

The Frog Prince
This famous fairy tale of love
and enchantment was among
those compiled in 1814 by
the Brothers Grimm, who
were contemporaries of Ernst
Hoffmann.

*There stood a beautiful
princess again.*

"So the friends sent
word of Crackatook to
the king and queen, who had already been
advertising for eligible young gentlemen with
strong teeth. They came from far and wide and there
were even one or two princes among them.

"The competition began, and, just as the astrologer had predicted,
all the gentlemen failed to crack Crackatook. One or two exhausted
competitors were even carried out by the court dentists. At last the
king was so fed up he offered his kingdom and Pirlipat's hand in
marriage to the man who could succeed. The astrologer then winked
at the clockmaker as if to say 'I told you so!'

"It was young Drosselmeier's turn to step forward. When Pirlipat
saw the handsome fellow she clasped her hands to her heart.

'Oh, let it be him!' she sighed longingly.

Young Drosselmeier picked up Crackatook and placed the nut
between his teeth. With two snaps, the shell shattered.

"He then courteously presented the kernel to the princess.

"As Pirlipat started eating the kernel, he closed his eyes and carefully began to take the seven magical steps backward, following the astrologer's instructions – one, two, three … The whole court fell silent. All eyes were on Pirlipat as she swallowed the last of the nut. Courtiers and servants gasped in unison – there stood a golden-haired princess again!

The trumpets sounded, the crowd cheered, and the queen, overcome with joy, fainted.

"But just as Drosselmeier took his seventh step backward, Dame Mouserink popped up through the floor. The heel of the young man's shoe spiked her neck and he stumbled. His body shrank, his head grew enormous, and his pigtail was replaced by a wooden cloak that worked his jaw. The handsome boy had become an ugly Nutcracker!

"Dame Mouserink lay squeaking horribly, '*Nutcracker, Nutcracker, you'll soon be dead, killed by my son with seven heads!*' With that, she died. She was unceremoniously picked up and carried out by the court stovelighter.

"Meanwhile the court was so busy admiring Pirlipat's restored beauty, and she so busy basking in the admiration, that all were oblivious to young Drosselmeier's fate. But then the princess reminded her father of his promise and the young man was brought forward. When she saw what had befallen the unfortunate hero, she hid her face in her hands.

'Papa!' she wailed. 'Get that hideous creature out of my sight!' Poor Nutcracker, the clockmaker, and the astrologer were banished.

"Yet the astrologer predicted that the spell could be broken – but only when the Mouse King had been killed and a lady had fallen in love with Nutcracker despite his ugliness.

"Dear Nutcracker, you must be my Godpapa's nephew."

Beastly beauty
Throughout history many people have thought that physical deformity and ugliness implied bad character. In Hoffmann's story, truth lies beneath surface appearances.

Chapter ten

UNCLE AND NEPHEW

"THERE," GRINNED DROSSELMEIER, finishing his story. "That was a hard nut to crack, but at least you know why nutcrackers are so ugly."

Marie sat up in bed, frowning. She was thoughtful for a moment, then she said sadly, "I think Pirlipat was horrid and ungrateful."

"If Nutcracker had been a real soldier," scoffed Fritz, "he'd have beaten the Mouse King and got back his looks."

Godpapa Drosselmeier just smiled to himself and said nothing.

Now a glass cut can be very nasty. Marie felt so dizzy that she had to stay in bed for a whole week. At last she felt better and jumped around as happily as before. She ran to the glass cabinet and peeped through the panes. The toys were fine, and there was Nutcracker with his teeth all perfectly in place.

Marie guessed that Godpapa Drosselmeier's story had been about himself and his feud with Dame Mouserink.

"Godpapa Drosselmeier and the clockmaker must be the same person," she thought as she looked at the silent Nutcracker.

"And, dear Nutcracker, you must be my Godpapa's nephew from Nuremberg. You should have married Pirlipat," she sighed. "In that case, you are the rightful King of Toyland," she told him, and then addressed the toys. "But you see, he is still under an evil spell – just like a prince from a fairy tale!"

Now that Marie had worked all this out, she expected the toys to show her they were alive. But they did nothing of the kind. They kept still in the cabinet.

"You can count on me, sweet Prince," whispered Marie, rather forlornly now, "and I'll ask Godpapa to help."

Nutcracker remained motionless, but Marie thought she heard a sigh from the cabinet and a familiar voice say,

"Marie so fair, like golden sunshine, I'll be yours if you'll be mine!"

She felt a thrill of delight tinged with apprehension.

That evening, the family had gathered for supper and Marie was sitting on her little stool by Godpapa Drosselmeier.

"I know that Nutcracker is really your nephew," she said to him, "so why don't you help him fight Mouserink's son?"

She then told them all about the battle between the toys and the mice.

"What a story!" laughed Mama.

"Utter nonsense," smiled Papa.

"My soldiers would never be such cowards," Fritz protested.

But Godpapa took Marie on his knee and whispered, "You have more power than us. You are a born princess, like Pirlipat. If you want to save Nutcracker, there are still many challenges facing you. You're the only one who can help him, so be faithful and true."

Time for supper
By 1800, children ate most meals with their parents. They sometimes drank out of child-sized cups and ate from child-sized plates. Supper or "tea" including fine cakes for wealthy families, was served at about six o'clock in the evening.

"Marie… You are a born princess, like Pirlipat."

candy
sticks

barley sugar

marzipan fruits
and shapes

sugar swan

chocolate
shapes

sugar mouse

Sweets and treats
*Wealthy children had a wide
choice of candy and
chocolate treats in 19th
century Germany. The sugar
figures were beautiful
confectionary designs which
children admired – and ate!*

*But that night the
Mouse King returned.*

One moonlit night, not long after this,
Marie was woken by a strange scratching
sound in the corner of her bedroom. She was
about to run to her mother to tell her that there
were mice in the house, when she saw the terrible
Mouse King pushing through a hole in the wall.
He jumped onto the table and hissed and squeaked.
"Give me your candy," he cried, "or I'll chew
Nutcracker into sawdust!" Marie froze with terror.

The next morning, still pale from fright, she didn't dare
tell Fritz or her mother and father what had happened,
because she was sure they would laugh at her again.
But Marie knew she had to help Nutcracker. So that night,
she left all her candy at the bottom of the cabinet.
When the sun rose the next day all the candy was bitten
and chewed up, except her marzipan, which the picky
Mouse King didn't like.

Marie didn't mind about her candy, simply feeling glad
that she had saved Nutcracker. But that night the
Mouse King returned. With a nasty gleam in his eye
he squeaked, "Give me your sugar toys!"

Marie was very sad as she put out her beautiful
collection of sugar toys. She kissed the shepherds
and shepherdesses, the jumping dog, the
sheep and the pretty Maid of Orleans.
But her most precious sugar toy was
a tiny girl with rosy cheeks.
When Marie thought of losing
this little one her eyes filled
with tears.

Nutcracker looked up
at her so pitifully, though,
that Marie decided she would
happily sacrifice *everything* to save him.

When Mrs. Drosselmeier saw the sad
remains of the sugar toys the next
morning, she was furious and told her
husband and Godpapa Drosselmeier
that mice had made a hole in the cabinet.

Fritz claimed that the baker's cat
downstairs could bite off the Mouse King's
head. But Mama was worried that a cat would
cause all sorts of mischief in the house, so Fritz
suggested that Godpapa Drosselmeier set one of the
traps he had invented. His parents laughed at this,
but Drosselmeier put his hand in his pocket and
pulled out a little box.

The children rushed downstairs to the kitchen,
and the cook started to brown some bacon to
put inside the trap.

"Be careful, Queen!" warned Marie as she
watched. "Remember the Mouserink family!"

But Fritz drew his toy sword and cried,
"Let them come – if they dare!"

When the fat was ready,
Drosselmeier fixed the browned
slab on a fine thread and set
the trap down gently in the
glass cabinet.

Chapter eleven

VICTORY

THAT NIGHT, as Marie lay in bed, she felt something cold running up her arm. The Mouse King was sitting on her shoulder, blood foaming from all his seven mouths.

"Stay out of that house, it's death to a mouse!" he hissed angrily.

Poor Marie was petrified.

"Now what's to do? Your picture books, too!" the Mouse King went on, spitefully.

"And I'll have your lace. By Nutcracker's face!"

Marie was brokenhearted at the thought of giving up her picture books and her pretty lace dress.

The next morning, her mother told her that they still had not caught the mouse and might have to get the baker's cat after all. Marie turned as white as a sheet and ran straight to the cabinet.

"Dear Nutcracker," she said. "What can I do? Even if I give all my picture books and my dress, the Mouse King will still ask for more. Soon I will have nothing left, and he will want to eat *me* and *you!*"

Marie was sobbing when she saw a spot of blood on Nutcracker's neck. It must have been there since the battle. She picked him up and wiped the blood away with her silk handkerchief.

Nutcracker immediately started growing warm in her hands and she put him down again. His jaw began to wobble.

"Dear Miss Stahlbaum," he whispered, "my true friend, I owe you so much. But don't give up your picture books and your dress for me. All I need is a sword. If you can get me one, I'll do the rest ..."

Nutcracker's voice died away. His eyes became as lifeless as before.

Marie's heart leapt for joy! She knew that she would not have to give up anything else. But where could she get a sword from?

She gently placed Nutcracker back on his shelf in the cabinet.

The Mouse King was sitting on Marie's shoulder, blood foaming from all his seven mouths.

A child's book-case from 1800

Picture books

Little Jack Horner, 1811 edition

Pretty as a picture
In the early 19th century, more advanced printing processes meant that books were richly illustrated in color and children had much more fun learning.

"I'll just have to talk to Fritz this evening, while Mama and Papa are out. I'll tell him everything," she resolved.

Ever since Marie had described the battle, Fritz had been very unhappy with the conduct of his hussars. When he heard the whole story, he shook his head and looked disapprovingly at the soldiers. Now, as a punishment, he took the plumes from their helmets and forbade them to sound their favorite March of the Hussars.

"As for a sword," he said, "I can help."

Fritz borrowed a silver saber from an old colonel, who was retired at the back of the shelf, and handed it to his sister. Marie sighed as she tied the little sword around Nutcracker's waist.

Graceful lace
Marie's lace dress probably came from Saxony, in Germany, where the lace-making industry flourished during the 19th century.

Marie tied the sword around Nutcracker's waist.

That night, Marie lay wide awake staring into the darkness. She could not sleep from worry. It wasn't until around midnight that she heard noises coming from behind the sitting-room doors. There was a rustling and a clanging, and suddenly a shrill *SQUEAK!*

"The King of Mice!" she cried, leaping out of bed in sheer terror.

But the room was quite silent. Marie held her breath and listened. Then there was a gentle tapping on the bedroom door and a voice she knew said softly, "Open the door, Miss Stahlbaum. Don't worry, there's good news."

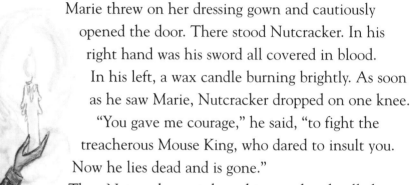

Nutcracker dropped on one knee.

Marie threw on her dressing gown and cautiously opened the door. There stood Nutcracker. In his right hand was his sword all covered in blood. In his left, a wax candle burning brightly. As soon as he saw Marie, Nutcracker dropped on one knee.

"You gave me courage," he said, "to fight the treacherous Mouse King, who dared to insult you. Now he lies dead and is gone."

Then Nutcracker put down his sword and pulled out the Mouse King's seven crowns. He held them out to Marie and continued, "Take these tokens of victory from one who is, until death, your true and faithful knight!"

Marie accepted them, speechless with delight.

"My beloved Miss Stahlbaum," begged Nutcracker, as he stood up, "if you will only follow me for just a few steps, I'll show you the most extraordinarily beautiful things. Come with me, dear lady!"

Marie did not hesitate for she knew that Nutcracker – or young Drosselmeier, as he must surely be – was a kind and honorable gentleman. And now that he was indebted to her, he would certainly keep his promise to show her wonders of all kinds.

"I will come with you, dear Mr. Drosselmeier," she answered, "but it can't be very far, or take very long, because you know I haven't had any sleep yet."

"Then we'll go by the shortest route!" cried Nutcracker. He turned and led Marie to the big, old wardrobe at the back of her bedroom. Marie was surprised to see that the doors, which were always shut, now stood wide open. Inside, her father's fox-fur traveling coat was hanging at the front.

Wonderful wardrobes
Another classic story that features a magical wardrobe is The Lion, the Witch, and the Wardrobe, by C.S. Lewis (published 1950). In the book, the wardrobe is a gateway to a wonderful world called Narnia.

*Up Marie
climbed…*

Nutcracker climbed
quickly up it and tugged on the
big tassel that hung down the back.

Immediately, a little cedarwood ladder
dropped down through one of the armholes and
Nutcracker told Marie to fear nothing, to have faith,
and follow him.

Up she climbed and, as her head emerged through the neck of the coat,
she was dazzled by a brilliant light streaming all around her.

Chapter twelve

LAND OF SWEETS

MARIE FOUND herself standing in a sweet-scented field. Sparks danced upward like glittering diamonds. "This is Candy Meadow," said Nutcracker, "but we'll go through that entrance over there."

Marie saw a wonderful gateway made of sugared almonds and raisins. There was a gallery running along the top of it that seemed to be made of barley sugar. Six monkeys in little red jackets sat there playing brass instruments.

Marie swept through the gate in a dream, only vaguely noticing that they were walking along a checkered marble pavement. She soon realized it was made out of different colored candies.

After a while, they found themselves in a glimmering wood. Gold and silver fruits hung from the trees, and ribbons and bows were draped around the branches. A gentle breeze was blowing, making the leaves tinkle and rustle like beautiful music.

"This is Christmas Wood," said Nutcracker.

"How lovely!" sighed Marie, "I wish I could stay here a little while."

Fairy-tale forests
The vast, brooding forests of southern Germany have inspired many artists and writers. This picture shows a beautiful Bavarian pine forest in wintertime.

With that, Nutcracker clapped his hands three times.

From the trees came graceful shepherds and shepherdesses, hunters and huntresses, so white that they seemed to be made out of sugar. They brought a beautiful golden chair with a white satin cushion and invited Marie to take a seat.

The shepherds and shepherdesses danced a pretty ballet for Marie, as the hunters and huntresses played their horns. Then they all took a bow and vanished again into the trees.

"I'm sorry it wasn't very good," said Nutcracker, "but these people are from the Clocktown Ballet Troupe, and they can only dance the same thing over and over again. Come on, Marie, we'd better be moving."

Soon they found themselves by a fragrant stream called Orange Brook. Nutcracker explained it wasn't nearly as beautiful as the great Lemonade River, which tumbles and foams into Almond Milk Sea. Indeed, a little later, Marie saw a swollen yellow river that went roaring and rushing along in a most refreshing way. Nearby, was a dark gold stream called Honeybrook. Boys and girls sat fishing there, and in the distance was a village called Sugarwell with houses that looked like gingerbread plastered with lemon peel and almonds.

"All the inhabitants of Sugarwell are very good-looking," explained Nutcracker, "but they're also bad-tempered because they've always got toothache. You can imagine why I suggest we don't go there."

Shepherds and shepherdesses danced a pretty ballet.

Tiny bird
The hummingbird is the world's smallest bird. It drinks nectar from flowers and most species have bright, iridescent plumage, ideal for small but spectacular headdresses.

Sweet paradise
Sugar-coated nuts, called comfits, were very popular in the early 19th century. Sweetmeats were small fancy cakes and pastries.

They then came to a town where thousands of people had gathered in the marketplace to unload carts that were piled high with packages of sticky, colored paper and slabs of chocolate.

"This is Bonbontown," explained Nutcracker. "And those carts are from Ribbonland. The King of Chocolate sent paper to fortify this town against attacks by the Fly Admiral. The chocolate is a gift."

Then they came to a wonderful, rose-scented lake where swans, all silvery white and wearing golden collars, glided back and forth. They were singing beautifully, while twinkling fish darted up and down through the rippling, rose-tinted water in time to the music.

"Oh!" cried Marie, happily. "This must be the lake Godpapa promised me once, and I am the girl who plays with the swans!"

But Nutcracker laughed. "I don't think my uncle could ever make such a beautiful thing!" he cried. "Come on, let's cross Lake Rosa."

He clapped his hands and a boat covered in precious stones and pulled by two golden-scaled dolphins came drifting towards them. Twelve African boys, with headdresses made of hummingbird's feathers, jumped out and carried the pair on board.

The nimble dolphins spouted jets of glittering crystal into the air.

Marie had just seen a pretty litle girl's face smiling up at her.

This annoyed the little African boys, who all opened umbrellas and started to stamp their feet. But Marie didn't notice this because she was gazing into the rosy waters, where she had just seen a pretty little girl's face smiling up at her.

"Look!" she gasped. "It's Princess Pirlipat!"

Nutcracker shook his head, and replied, with amusement,

"No, dear Miss Stahlbaum, that isn't Princess Pirlipat. It's only your own lovely face smiling back at you from the water."

Marie pulled back immediately and felt very ashamed.

They had reached the far shore now and the boys carried them into a gorgeous, sweetly perfumed grove, almost more wonderful than Christmas Wood.

"This is Comfit Grove," said Nutcracker proudly, "and over there lies the great metropolis of Sweetmeat City."

Oh, what a fabulous sight! In front of Marie stretched a magnificent city with colored walls and towers spiralling, twisting, curling and curving in wonderful shapes. Instead of roofs, the houses wore intertwining crowns and the towers were carved with delicate leaves. The gate seemed to be made of sugared fruits and macaroons, and a little squad of silver soldiers presented arms as the group entered. A man in a brocade jacket ran up to them.

"Welcome home, dear Prince!" he cried to Nutcracker. "Welcome home to Sweetmeat City!"

The square was
crowded with delightful
little people.

Brahmin priests in prayer.

Turkish delights?
*In real life, a mogul was a
Turkish king and janissaries
were his bodyguards.
Brahmins were Indian
priests. Hoffmann adds
these characters to his story
to make Sweetmeat City
even more exotic.*

Chapter thirteen

THE METROPOLIS

BEYOND THE WALLS was a great marketplace lined with sugar
houses. An obelisk – actually a giant frosted cake – spouted
fountains of lemonade. The square was crowded with
delightful little people, shouting, laughing, and singing.

The noise grew louder because the Great Mogul, attended by
seven hundred slaves, was crossing the square. Five hundred
fishermen had set up their stalls nearby and, at that moment, the
Grand Turk, with three thousand janissaries, decided to cross, too.
There was so much pushing and shoving that everybody started
fighting and one of the fishermen knocked off a brahmin's head.

A man suddenly shouted "Pastrycook!" three times, and everyone
fell silent. Nutcracker explained that "Pastrycook" meant a terrible,
unknown power that represented the ultimate fate of these people.
The word always silenced a noisy crowd.

But now Marie cried out in astonishment. She saw a beautiful rosy white castle shining with hundreds of towers. Bright exotic flowers bloomed from every wall.

"Welcome to Marzipan Castle," smiled Nutcracker. Marie noticed that one of the main towers was missing its sparkling roof. Nutcracker told her that the Giant Sweet Tooth had been passing one day and had bitten it off – much to the inhabitants' dismay!

Then Marie heard beautiful music as twelve pages with heads made of pearls and bodies of emeralds and rubies ran out of the castle. Behind them were four ladies, about the size of Miss Clara, but dressed so wonderfully that Marie knew they must be princesses.

"Dear Prince, our beloved brother!" they wept in joy.

"This is Miss Stahlbaum," said Nutcracker, introducing Marie, "daughter of the good Dr. Stahlbaum. She saved my life by throwing her shoe at the Mouse King and finding me a sword. Can Pirlipat, though a princess, ever compare with her?"

"Oh no!" they cried. Hugging Marie, they led her inside.

The castle rooms were made of crystal and full of the most perfect little furniture. The princesses sat Marie and Nutcracker down and told them there would be a banquet. They gathered fruits, spices, and sugar almonds, and began to prepare the feast.

Marie was thinking how much she would like to help when Nutcracker's youngest sister, as if she had read Marie's thoughts, handed her a little golden mortar and pestle.

"Dear friend, my brother's savior," she smiled, "would you mind crushing some sugar candy?"

Flat or fizzy?
Lemonade and orangeade in the early 19th century were cloudy and tangy but not bubbly. Drinks were carbonated only from the late 19th century. Sherbet was a favorite bubbly treat for children and adults.

"Dear Prince, our beloved brother!"

Marie started grinding the candy while Nutcracker told the whole story of the battle with the Mouse King. His voice and the sound of the mortar were like a beautiful, low chant which grew fainter. Suddenly, a silvery mist descended like clouds in which the pages and the princesses and Nutcracker and Marie herself began to float. They rose higher and higher until – *whooosh!* – Marie felt herself falling, falling ...

When she opened her eyes she was in bed again and her mother was standing over her.

"You've had a long sleep," she said softly. "Up you get now, little one, breakfast is ready."

Marie told her everything she had seen in the Land of Sweets.

"What a beautiful dream!" agreed her mother, amused.

Marie knew that it wasn't a dream and that she must have fallen asleep in Marzipan Castle and been carried home by the pages. She went on insisting, until her mother took her to the cabinet and pulled out the nutcracker.

"Silly girl," she smiled, "how could this bit of wood be alive?"

When Marie answered that she knew he was young Drosselmeier, both her parents burst out laughing. They laughed and laughed until Marie ran back into her bedroom and grabbed the Mouse King's seven crowns.

Mortar and pestle

Crushing candy
Mortars and pestles for grinding food are still used in the kitchen today. The mortar is the hard bowl, often made of stone, and the pestle is the grinding tool.

Nutcracker, the princesses, and Marie rose higher and higher.

"There," she said proudly, "there's the proof!"

Her parents looked at the crowns in amazement. They really were very beautiful and made out of a metal her parents had never seen before. Papa demanded to know where Marie had really got them. He listened and then scolded her for lying. Marie burst into tears.

The door opened and in came Godpapa Drosselmeier.

"Hello!" he cried cheerfully. "Why is my little Marie so unhappy?"

Dr. Stahlbaum explained and showed him the crowns.

"Stuff and nonsense," said Drosselmeier. "They're the crowns from my watch chain. I gave them to Marie for her second birthday. Don't you remember?"

None of them *did* remember, but now Marie ran up to him.

"Godpapa," she begged, "tell them I'm not lying. Tell them Nutcracker is really your nephew and he gave me the crowns!"

"Rubbish!" answered Drosselmeier crossly.

Papa told Marie that if she didn't stop lying he'd throw all her toys – and Nutcracker – out of the window.

"Godpapa," Marie begged, "tell them I'm not lying!"

Charming chains

In the 19th century, wealthy women often wore pretty chains called chatelaines at their waists. These held keys, watches, and little trinkets. Silver charm bracelets are worn today for good luck.

19th-century chatelaine

lucky charm bracelet

silver spoon and eggcup

Fairy godmothers?

Parents may choose "godparents" for their children. These are a child's special guardians who often give their godchild a silver gift when he or she is born.

"Loyal and lovely Marie!" he cried.

Chapter fourteen

CONCLUSION

MARIE DIDN'T DARE SAY ANOTHER WORD. Fritz made a face at her. Then he gave his hussars back their plumes and let them sound the march again. The memories of her adventures haunted Marie for months and months. Instead of playing as she used to, she would sit quietly and think wistfully to herself; everyone called her "Marie, the dreamer."

But one day, Godpapa Drosselmeier was fixing one of the clocks in the house and Marie was gazing at Nutcracker.

"Dear Nutcracker," she said suddenly, "if you really were alive I wouldn't hate you like Pirlipat does. You had to sacrifice your fine looks, and I truly love and respect you."

"Stuff and nonsense!" muttered Drosselmeier.

All of a sudden there was a tremendous flash, a loud bang, and Marie tumbled off her chair.

She came to and saw her mother fussing around her.

"Marie, you're too big to be falling off your chair," she scolded.

"Now, darling, look who's here. Godpapa Drosselmeier's nephew from Nuremberg."

Marie looked up and saw her godfather holding a very small but handsome gentleman by the hand. He was wearing a fine red coat, white stockings and a powdered wig with a pigtail. There was a jeweled sword at his side.

He delighted Marie by giving her a box of dainty sugar toys, just like those the Mouse King had eaten. And he gave Fritz a beautiful saber. At supper he even cracked the hardest nuts for the children by putting them in his mouth and tugging his pigtail.

Marie blushed whenever she looked at the elegant young man.

"Now children, play nicely together," said Godpapa with a smile.

But as soon as they were alone, the young man fell on one knee.

"Loyal and lovely Marie!" he cried. "I am young Drosselmeier, whose life you saved. I thank you with all my heart for loving me

Portrait of Master Day, by Gilbert Stuart, c.1790

19th-century boy's sword

Stylish sweetheart
At this time, boys from wealthy families wore formal, elaborate clothes. When a boy was 12 years old, he was often presented with a small sword.

Marie is still queen of a glittering kingdom.

despite my ugliness, for now the evil spell is broken – I am no longer a nutcracker! Marie, will you marry me and be Queen of the Sweetmeat Kingdom?"

"Dear Mr. Drosselmeier," Marie replied graciously, "you are good and kind, and you rule a delightful people. Yes, I accept your hand."

So they were engaged and, after a year and a day (or thereabouts), the young king arrived at her house one morning in a golden coach drawn by silver horses. The royal bride and bridegroom galloped away in bright sunshine. A thousand dolls danced at their wedding, and Marie is still queen of a glittering kingdom of Christmas Woods and Marzipan Castles; a kingdom where you can see all kinds of wonderful things – if you look with the right eyes!

Golden wedding

Golden coaches are not just creations of fairy-tale fantasy. Since the Middle Ages, European kings and queens have ridden in them to royal coronations and weddings.

Gold coach of Queen Elizabeth II

FROM BOOK TO BALLET

The Nutcracker in a recent Atlanta Ballet production.

In 1891, the Imperial Theater of St. Petersburg commissioned the Russian composer Peter Tchaikovsky to write the music for their new ballet based on Hoffmann's story. It was the first ballet in which children played important characters: the Stahlbaum children in the first scene, and mice, candy, or soldiers in the rest. *The Nutcracker* was a huge success, and some of the most famous dancers and directors of all time have since staged the ballet. It continues to enchant audiences at Christmas time all around the world.

Peter Ilyich Tchaikovsky (1840–93)

St. Petersburg was a center of Russian art and culture; the theater was at its heart.

His music for Swan Lake (1877), Sleeping Beauty (1890), and The Nutcracker are the best-loved of all ballet scores.

Sugar Plum Fairy

In the third act of the ballet, the Sugar Plum Fairy dances in the Land of Sweets. The twinkling melody for this is played on a celesta. Tchaikovsky discovered the celesta on a trip to Paris, and was the first composer to use it in a ballet.

The celesta is a small keyboard instrument with very bright tones.

Anna Pavlova

In the ballet, Marie is renamed Clara. One of the most famous 20th-century ballerinas, Anna Pavlova, danced the role of Clara in a 1912 production at the Palace Theatre, London.

Leticia Müller dances a "pas de deux" with Wolfgang Stollwitzer in the Birmingham Royal Ballet production in 1998.

Alexandre Benois' enchanting set design for the Land of Sweets in a 1957 production in London.

Sweet sets
Hoffmann was himself a stage designer. The landscapes in his story, such as the Land of Sweets and the Christmas Woods, adapt easily for the stage.

In the ballet, Clara (Marie) is given ballet shoes for Christmas, which she dances in.

A dainty Clara performs a lovely arabesque as she dances with her beloved Nutcracker.

Graceful godpapa
Joseph Cipolla of the Birmingham Royal Ballet was Godpapa Drosselmeier in the 1998 production. He turned the character into an elegant but sinister magician.

The Dance of the Snowflakes in the English National Ballet production of 1998.

A member of the Royal Ballet dances the role of the evil Mouse King.

HOFFMANN AND HIS TIMES

Ernst Hoffmann had a gift for showing how dreams invade real life. He lived through the Napoleonic Wars (1799–1815) in a time of many scientific discoveries. His own life contained many tragedies. In his stories, Hoffmann creates childlike worlds of magic and fantasy to illuminate these realities. His work was inspired by composers as well as other writers, and his vision has influenced musicians and authors since his early death.

A German edition of The Nutcracker

The city of Königsberg was the cultural center of East Prussia. Hoffmann studied law at the university and became a judge there in 1795.

Living through nightmares

Hoffmann was born in 1776 in Königsberg. He married Mischa Rohrer in 1802. After the death of their baby daughter, Mischa had an accident, which left her very ill. Hoffmann, himself, died in 1822, aged only 46.

Plume worn by officers, sergeants, and buglers

Napoleon I (1769 – 1821), the powerful and ambitious Emperor of France

WAR WITNESS

Hoffmann lived in Dresden and Leipzig, in the Prussian empire, between 1813 and 1815, where he composed music. In these cities he witnessed battles between the Prussian armies and the French armies lead by Napoleon. In letters to friends, he vividly described the colorful squadrons of hussars and the sound of cannon fire – details echoed in The Nutcracker.

Telescope used to scan the vast battlefields

Soldiers used compasses for reconnaissance work.

Woes of war

The terror which made Nutcracker's soldiers retreat from the enemy reflects the experiences of many soldiers on the battlefields of Prussia.

Rifle

Cartridge box for ammunition

Battle of Leipzig, 1813

Hoffmann was in the city during this famous battle, where the Prussians defeated the French.

FLIGHTS OF FANCY

Hoffmann's time saw many scientific advances, but none fired the public's imagination more than the hot-air balloon and the magic lantern. Both inventions opened up wonderful possibilities, blurring the boundary between science and fantasy.

To the moon in a balloon?

In 1783, the Montgolfier brothers made the first successful flight in a balloon. The potential for human flight suddenly seemed limitless.

Magic lantern

Hoffmann said that his vivid imagination worked like a magic lantern. This projected images, painted on slides, onto a screen using candle or gas light.

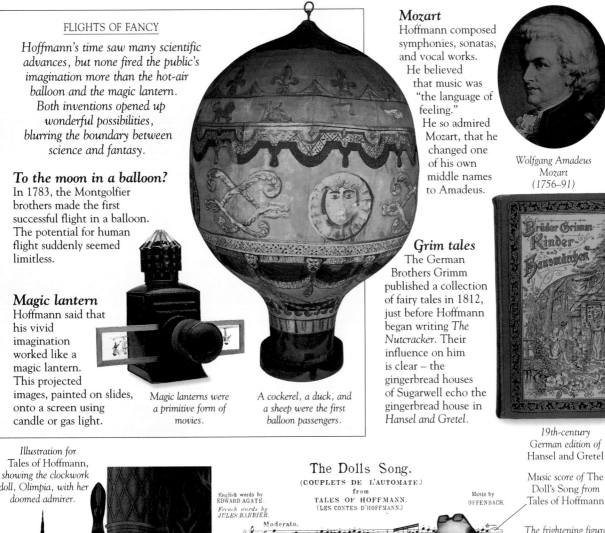

Magic lanterns were a primitive form of movies.

A cockerel, a duck, and a sheep were the first balloon passengers.

Mozart

Hoffmann composed symphonies, sonatas, and vocal works. He believed that music was "the language of feeling." He so admired Mozart, that he changed one of his own middle names to Amadeus.

Wolfgang Amadeus Mozart (1756–91)

Grim tales

The German Brothers Grimm published a collection of fairy tales in 1812, just before Hoffmann began writing *The Nutcracker*. Their influence on him is clear – the gingerbread houses of Sugarwell echo the gingerbread house in *Hansel and Gretel*.

19th-century German edition of Hansel and Gretel

Illustration for Tales of Hoffmann, showing the clockwork doll, Olimpia, with her doomed admirer.

The Dolls Song.

(COUPLETS DE L'AUTOMATE.)

from
TALES OF HOFFMANN.
(LES CONTES D'HOFFMANN.)

English words by
EDWARD AGATE.

French words by
JULES BARBIER.

Music by
OFFENBACH.

Music score of The Doll's Song from Tales of Hoffmann

The frightening figure of Coppelius from Tales of Hoffmann, staged at London's Royal Opera House in 1992.

The magical tale-spinner

The German composer Jacques Offenbach (1819-1880) based his grand opera *Tales of Hoffmann* on Hoffmann's most famous stories. The central figure was Ernst himself, whom Offenbach portrayed as a magician-like character. The opera was produced in 1881, a year after the death of its composer.

Acknowledgments

Picture Credits

The publishers would like to thank the following for their kind permission to reproduce the photographs.

t=top, b=bottom, l=left, r=right, a=above, c=center

AKG London Ltd: 2, 8tl, 8c, 8cr, 8cl, 9bl, 9bc, 9c, 9ca, 24bl, 28cl, 38tl, 60bl, 62ca, 62br.
Atlanta Ballet Company/Kim Kenney: 60tl.
Birmingham Royal Ballet/Bill Cooper: 60c, 61cr.
The Bowes Museum, Barnard Castle: 11c.
Bridgeman Art Library: 10tl, 12bl, 33c, 35br, 42bl, 47tl, 57ar, 58cl, 62cl.
Christie's Images: 10br, 11bl, 11br, 46bl.
Dee Conway: 7.
Andy Crawford Photography: 25tr, 29br, 44tl, 52tcl, 55tr. With thanks to David and Gisela Barrington, 'Yesterday Child', London: 10c, 10ca, and Judith Lassalle, London: 11tr.
Bethnal Green/V & A Museum Picture Library: 18tl.
Kit Houghton/HM The Queen: 59tr.
Florence Nightingale Museum/Geoff Dann: 26tl.
Green Jackets/Winchester/Geoff Dann: 62cr, 62ar.

95th Rifles/Private Collection/Geoff Brightling: 23trb, 62bl.
Washington Doll's House & Toy Museum/Matthew Ward: 30tl.
Alex Wilson/Williamson Collection: 56bl.
English National Ballet/Catherine Ashmore: 60/61, 61ca.
ET Archive: 31tr, 34bl, 54bl, 61tl, 61br, 62tl.
Mary Evans Picture Library: 11tl, 37tr, 40tl, 40bl, 60tc, 63cr, 63bl.
Robert Harding: 9tl.
Hulton Getty Picture Collection: 60tr, 63tr.
Performing Arts Library/Clive Barda: 63br.
Power Stock/Zefa: 50bl.
Science & Society Picture Library: 63tc.
Science Museum: 27cr, 27br.
Sotheby's Picture Library: 10cr.
Tony Stone Images: 15br.
V & A Picture Library: 11cl, 28bl, 46cl.

Additional photography by: Andy Crawford, Lynton Gardiner, Steve Gorton, Barnabas Kindersley, Dave King, Liz McCaulay, Diana Miller, David Murray, Karl Shone, Matthew Ward Barrie Watts.

Dorling Kindersley would particularly like to thank curators at the Bethnal Green Museum of Childhood for their assistance.